Lilly
and the
Ladybirds

Damon Burnard

h
Hodder
Children's
Books

Por mi vida, Maria

Published as a My First Read Alone
in Great Britain in 2000
by Hodder Children's Books

10 9 8 7 6 5 4 3 2

ISBN 0 340 78780 5

Printed and bound by Omnia Books Ltd, Glasgow

Hodder Children's Books
a division of Hodder Headline Limited
338 Euston Road
London NW1 3BH

Visit Damon's website!
http://home1.gte.net/dburnard

Lilly, the little blue bug, lived in a beautiful garden. Can you find her house?

Here's a clue: it's on a sunflower leaf!

One morning, Lilly looked out of her window.

She watched the bright butterflies, and the colourful caterpillars playing.

And then she looked in the mirror.

'There's nothing special about me at all!' she sighed. 'Who'd want to play with me?'

Lilly went into the kitchen.
Her mum was baking a cake.

'Lilly, dear?' asked her mum.
'Can you pick me a rose petal for
my cake?'

'Do I have to?' asked Lilly.
She was afraid of the caterpillars
and butterflies making fun of her.

'It would be a great help, dear,'
said her mum.

And it's a
lovely day
outside!

Lilly loved rose petal cake . . .

. . . so off she flew to the rosebush.

Lilly picked a tiny petal.
Suddenly she saw three ladybirds
sitting on a leaf.

'Wow!' gasped Lilly.

They're beautiful!

She watched them talking
and laughing.

Lilly wished that she could join in,
but she flew home instead.

'They'd never want to play with a plain blue bug like me!' she thought.

Lilly gave the petal to her mum . . .

. . . and went to her room.

'I wish I had a lovely black and red coat!' Lilly sighed. 'I bet they'd play with me if I did!'

Then Lilly had an idea.

She grabbed her paints and a big, bushy brush . . .

. . . opened a pot of red . . .

. . . and started to paint her back!

It wasn't easy!

As hard as she tried, Lilly couldn't reach the middle.

'It's no use!' she moaned.

But then Lilly had another idea.

She went outside . . .

. . . and found a big leaf.

'What's that for, Lilly?' asked
her mum.
'Oh, nothing!' said Lilly.

She painted the leaf red . . .

. . . and made six black blobs.

And then Lilly did the STRANGEST thing . . .

She lay down on top of it!

Lilly jumped up and looked in the mirror.

'It worked!' she squealed.

The red and black paint had stuck to her back!

When her mum wasn't looking . . .

. . . Lilly tiptoed outside.

Off she flew to the rosebush.

The ladybirds were still there!

'Here goes!' thought Lilly.

She took a deep breath and flew
down.

'Hello!' said Lilly, as she landed.

The three ladybirds turned round.

'Who are you?' they asked.

'I'm Lilly, the ladybird,' said Lilly, the little blue bug.

'Hi, Lilly!' said one ladybird. 'My name is Ruby! And this is Scarlet, and Crimson!'

'Hi, Lilly!' said Scarlet and Crimson.

'Hi,' said Lilly. 'I'm pleased to meet you.'

'Would you like to play with us?'
asked Ruby.

'Who, me?' asked Lilly.
'Yes, YOU!' laughed Ruby.

'YES, PLEASE!' said Lilly.

First they played hide and seek . . .

. . . then they played hopscotch . . .

. . . then they skipped . . .

. . . and then they played tag.

It was ever so much fun!

'Phew!' said Ruby, at last.

'Me, too!' said Lilly, and Scarlet, and Crimson.

They all sat down to rest.

Together they talked, and laughed, and sang . . .

Lilly was having so much fun, she didn't notice a little raincloud, floating across the sky . . .

. . . and she didn't notice the raindrops starting to fall . . .

Suddenly the ladybirds stopped talking and laughing.

They stared at Lilly instead.

'What is it?' asked Lilly.
'YOU!' gasped Scarlet.

Lilly was standing in a red and
black puddle!

The rain was washing the paint away!

'You're not a ladybird!' cried Ruby.
'You're BLUE!' gasped Crimson.

Lilly screamed . . .

. . . and she jumped off the leaf.

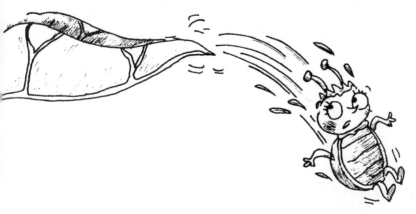

'COME BACK!' shouted Ruby.

But Lilly was gone.

'Where have you been?' asked her mum, when Lilly got home. 'I've been worried!'

'Oh, Mum!' said Lilly, and she started to cry.

'There, there!' said her mum.
'Tell me all about it.'

Lilly told her about the ladybirds,
and about the paint . . . and about
the raindrops.

'Oh, silly Lilly!' said her mum.
'You're the most beautiful bug
in the whole, wide world!'

'No I'm not!' wept Lilly. 'I'm just
small, and blue, and very plain!'

She ran to her room and slammed
the door shut.

'They'll never want to play with me, now!' she sobbed. 'Not ever, ever again!'

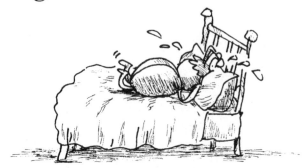

Suddenly . . .

KNOCK! KNOCK!

There was a knock at the door!

'Go away!' said Lilly.

'But, Lilly,' said her mum . . .

It was the ladybirds!

'It's me!' called Scarlet. 'And Ruby, and Crimson! Can we please come in?'

'Hmmph!' thought Lilly. 'They've come to make fun of me! Well, I don't care any more!'

Lilly opened the door.

'Here I am!' she said. 'Now laugh all you want!'

But nobody laughed.

The ladybirds rushed over to Lilly.

Lilly looked at her feet.

'I didn't think you'd play with a bug like me!' she said.

And THEN the ladybirds laughed!

'Oh, Lilly!' said Ruby. 'We don't care what you look like!'

'Besides,' said Crimson, 'blue is a beautiful colour!'

'Really?' asked Lilly.
'Really!' said the ladybirds.

'I'm glad that's settled!' Lilly's mum smiled.

'Now, who'd like a slice of rose petal cake?'

The cake was delicious!

When they were all full up, Lilly showed the ladybirds how she'd painted her back.

They thought she was very clever!

'Hey, Lilly!' said Scarlet,

'No!' said Crimson,

'Paint me blue!' said Ruby.

Lilly and the ladybirds painted themselves all the colours of the rainbow . . .

They played for hours, until it was time to go home . . .

The ladybirds asked Lilly if she could play tomorrow. And be their friend for ever.

'Yes, please!' said Lilly.

It took a while for Lilly to clean up her room . . .

. . . and even longer to clean up herself.

And then she looked in the mirror.

A little blue bug was looking back at her. And the little blue bug was smiling.

'Yes!' thought Lilly, 'I look good in blue! Very good, indeed!'